Little, Brown and Company

Hachette Book Group
237 Park Avenue, New York, NY 10017
Visit our website at lb-kids.com

LB kids is an imprint of Little, Brown and Company.
The LB kids name and logo are trademarks of Hachette Book Group, Inc.

The publisher is not responsible for websites (or their content) that are not owned by the publisher.

First Edition: March 2014

Library of Congress Control Number: 2013955924

ISBN 978-0-316-28331-1

10 9 8 7 6 5 4 3 2 1

CW

Printed in the United States of America

Adventure at Skull Rock

Adapted by Kirsten Mayer
Illustrated by the Disney Storybook Art Team

LITTLE, BROWN & COMPANY
LB kids

Zarina is a dust-keeper fairy who lives in Pixie Hollow. But Zarina is not content just wrapping up the golden pixie dust, which helps fairies fly. She wonders what else pixie dust can do.

One day, she works with the very special Blue Dust. Just a tiny bit makes the golden pixie dust multiply!

Zarina has been experimenting with pixie dust at home. Now she figures out that a speck of Blue Dust supercharges her experiments—and turns golden pixie dust different colors!

Zarina spills some pink dust on a little plant—and the plant grows so big and so fast that it destroys part of Pixie Hollow! The dust-keeper fairy in charge tells Zarina that she's no longer allowed to work at the Dust Depot.

Sad, Zarina packs her things and flies away. She isn't seen in Pixie Hollow for a long time....

One year later, the fairies of Pixie Hollow are celebrating the Four Seasons Festival. But while all the fairies watch the show...

...someone sneaks in and steals all the Blue Pixie Dust! Without the magic dust, the fairies won't be able to make golden pixie dust, which means they won't be able to fly anymore.

Tinker Bell says she saw Zarina before the show and wonders if she took the dust.

"What could she want it for?" asks Silvermist.

"I don't know, but we have to find her!"cries Tink.

Tinker Bell and her friends, Vidia, Silvermist, Rosetta, Fawn, and Iridessa, set off to follow Zarina.

Fawn spots a blue glow up ahead. "Over there!" she cries.

"Come on," says Tink. "We've got to find that dust."
The fairies follow Zarina's path through the woods and
finally reach the coast. They see a pirate ship!

The fairies find Zarina on the ship and grab the sack of Blue Pixie Dust from her.
"Give me back that dust!" yells Zarina. She chases them back to shore.
"This dust belongs to Pixie Hollow!" cries Tinker Bell.

The rogue fairy takes a handful of multicolored dust from her satchel and throws it over the other fairies. The force of the magic dust knocks them backward—and through a waterfall!

Zarina grabs the Blue Dust and flies away.

As they stand up and shake themselves off, the fairies realize that Zarina's dust switched their powers!

Now Tinker Bell has a water talent. Silvermist has a fast-flying talent. Vidia has a tinker talent. Rosetta has an animal talent. Iridessa has a garden talent, and Fawn has a light talent.

The fairies sneak up and spy on the pirates.

"You gotta love the boots," whispers Rosetta, noting Zarina's new look.

"Shhhhh!" scolds Tink. She wants to hear what Zarina and the pirates are saying.

A pirate named James is giving a toast to Zarina.

"Just one year ago, we'd lost everything...and then we found her." James nods at Zarina. "We needed a captain. And when we humbly asked if she could make us fly..."

The fairies gasp at James's words. Zarina has become a pirate captain! Even more shocking, she plans to make the *whole pirate ship fly*!

The pirates cheer as the ship sails toward a scary cave called Skull Rock.

At Skull Rock, the fairies spot something that looks familiar.

"It looks like..." starts Iridessa.

"...the Pixie Dust Tree back home!" finishes Rosetta.

"Zarina must have grown it," adds Silvermist.

"So that's how they're going to fly: She's going to make pixie dust!" Tink exclaims.

Zarina will be able to create lots of golden pixie dust by pouring some of the Blue Dust she stole into the tree.

The fairies hide and watch as Zarina carries the Blue Dust up into the Pixie Dust Tree.

"As soon as she's gone, we'll grab the dust and get out of here," says Vidia.

"Maybe we should try to talk to her," says Tink.

"That didn't work out at the waterfall," Vidia says, disagreeing.

A bee starts to buzz around Iridessa. "Shoo!" she whispers.

Trying to get away from the bee, Iridessa knocks into a branch. Her touch gives it a growth spurt! The branch shoots out toward Zarina, taking all the girls with it!

Zarina is surprised, but she quickly points her sword at the girls and whistles.

The pirates swoop in and nab the fairies with a fishing net.

Tinker Bell cries out, "Zarina, don't do this! Come back home!"

Zarina laughs. "I'll never go back to Pixie Hollow!" she vows.

But once the tree starts making golden pixie dust, James turns on the tiny pirate fairy and locks her in a lantern!

"We don't need you anymore! Our plan worked perfectly!" James laughs. "With a flying ship, there's no stopping us!"

He tosses Zarina and the lantern overboard. "Bon voyage, little captain!"

James was just using Zarina's talent. He was never her friend!

Tink and the girls escape the net and hurry off the ship. They see the lantern with Zarina inside. The lantern is starting to sink.

"Help me!" cries Zarina. The fairies zoom over to rescue her.

"I'm so sorry," Zarina says.

Tinker Bell smiles warmly at her. The group forgives their old friend. Now it's time to stop those pirates!

The fairies arm themselves with tiny hatpins and prepare to fight the pirates.

They demand the pirates return the dust, but the pirates just laugh at the tiny fairies. The pirates don't believe they can be hurt by such small foes, but they are in for a big surprise!

"Our talents!" shouts Tinker Bell to her friends.

The girls work together using their new talents to stop the ship and knock the pirates overboard.

James sprinkles golden dust on himself and tries to fly away. But Zarina sees one speck of Blue Dust and hurls it at the pirate. The Blue Dust mixes with the gold dust and multiplies it. James flies out of control, right into a big wave of water. Tink sent the wave using her new water talent.

"Can't fly when you're wet!" cries Zarina. "Good-bye, James!"

The fairies have won! They head home to Pixie Hollow.

"Queen Clarion, we got the Blue Dust back!" cries Tinker Bell. "We also got Zarina!"

"Well then, the Blue Dust isn't the most valuable thing you brought back to me today," says the queen. She welcomes Zarina home and invites her to show off her new pixie dust alchemy talent.

Zarina smiles at her friends. She is happy to be home.